LITTLE GREEN MEN

CURTIS BASS

Published by Water Dragon Publishing
waterdragonpublishing.com

ISBN 978-1-959804-82-6 (Trade Paperback)

FIRST EDITION

10 9 8 7 6 5 4 3 2 1

LITTLE GREEN MEN

LIEUTENANT CALEB COOPER

"**B**URKE! MOVE YOUR ASS. We're on a timeline here," Gilmore barked.

There he goes, showing his ass again. I wish he'd just lay off.

"Ignore him," I whispered, my face close to Burke's ear as I worked on his helmet. Louder, I said, "Hold yer damn horses, Cap. His communicator is going wonky. I'll be finished quick as a duck on a June bug. Mars ain't going nowhere."

"Two months of taking his shit is more than a man should have to stomach," Burke ground through gritted teeth.

"Just think of the fame," I soothed. "First men on Mars. It's worth taking a little shit, even from two gorillas." I kept my voice low. Lieutenant Colonel Jim Gilmore was only three feet away, half in the lander. I thought Gilmore looked rather comical with just his upper body visible, as if someone had sliced the lower half off. "Remember, we smart guys got to stick together. Go get 'em, Papa Bear."

I patted Burke's helmet top. I was always amused at the pink flush that crept over his cheeks and suppressed grin whenever I called him that. Burke was good people, as we say back home. Not like those two flyboys suffering from testosterone poisoning. He and I had really connected on the flight from Earth. We conspired together as the two brains against the two boneheads. We had special looks and inside jokes, always at Gilmore's expense. We were seventeen years apart, however, so there was a definite generational shift. He was the staid Boston Yankee to my Georgia country boy.

"Good to go." I called.

Gilmore disappeared down the hole in the floor, Burke clambering down after, the landing suit, while not bulky, still making him clumsy. Once he was in, they sealed the entrance.

"Separation is a go. Y'all go find some Martians," I said into my communication device.

The orbiter craft shuddered as the lander broke away. I floated over to a porthole sized window to see the craft fall away. Not being fond of the weightlessness here in the central axis of the *Liberty*, I pulled myself hand over hand to the torus. The control room, labs and sleeping quarters were in the torus, which spun around the docking port in the axis, the rotation providing one Earth G.

One entire week alone. Sweet home Alabama, that will be heaven! Though gregarious by nature, I was going to relish some privacy after living cheek by jowl like grandpa's pigs with the other three men for two months. *Peace and quiet and no more of that tension between Burke and Cap. Well, this is Burke's time to shine. Being a geologist, he has felt useless for most of the mission. But now he is on his way down to the planet to do what he was trained for.*

"Give 'em what for, Papa Bear," I whispered.

MAJOR DAVID BURKE

I'm freaking going down to Mars. Fucking Mars! I'm in the books now. Everyone throughout history will know my name.

I had worked toward this for years. When I hit forty, I was afraid I was too old for a space mission, but I made first alternate geologist. Even at the "advanced age" of forty-five. One lucky broken foot, and I was on my way. *Oh shit, I hope I don't barf.*

"Five hundred meters," Major Jeff Toms, the pilot, called out.

The oblong landing craft was just wide enough for three reclining seats, which would be our workstations and beds for the next week.

"Three hundred."

Our feet were against one end of the craft and there was enough space between the seats to sidle over to the square meter of open space behind. At six one, Lieutenant Colonel Gilmore could just stand erect.

"One hundred."

Thick triangular shaped windows looked out on either side of the craft. I could see mountains, misty and pink in the distance. *The Mountains of Mars*. I looked over at Major Toms, gripping the controls, sweat making his black face glisten.

"Fifty meters," he continued his countdown.

A few moments later, I felt the craft come to rest on the planet. *We are on Mars!* My stomach was turning somersaults in the one-third Earth gravity. I fought back the nausea, knowing throwing up now would just make me a laughingstock to the two jocks I was stuck with.

"Welcome to Mars. The captain has turned off the seatbelt sign. Feel free to move about the cabin," Toms joked.

"Perfect landing, Jeff. Just as expected," Gilmore said.

"Fucking A!" Toms yelled. "Mars, we are here!" He raised both hands up, palms out. Gilmore on his right and I on his left slapped his hands.

"Hell yeah," Gilmore added, with fervor in his voice.

"How y'all doin' down they-ah?" Cooper's syrupy drawl came over the radio from some three hundred miles above us.

"All systems normal, Coop. You mind the store and keep the comm open," Gilmore responded.

"Will do. Over and out, Cap," Cooper responded.

Gilmore opened a channel on his comm unit. "Houston, this is *Freedom* calling from Planitia Base. Greetings from the Red Planet. Over." He turned off the unit. "Well, I expect an answer in about sixteen minutes given the distance. Now, I want a full check of all systems while we wait, Jeff. Burke, get below and check that the equipment and storage bins are still secure. They could have shifted during descent."

We began our assigned duties, coordinating our movements in the tight landing module. Behind the seats was enough room to get into and out of the EVA suits one at a time. Also aft was a hatch giving entrance to the lower module. As in the old lunar exploration days, we would leave the lower part of the lander behind when we had completed our mission. I unlatched the hatch and climbed down into the bottom unit.

"Everything's five by five, Cap," Toms reported, meaning all the systems were operating within acceptable limits.

Meanwhile, I checked to make sure all the equipment we would need for our EVAs was secure. Once I'd ensured all the instruments were working and feeding data up to *Liberty*, I climbed back up to the command module.

"Good. What's it look like outside?" Gilmore asked. The cameras would provide a better view than the thick windows.

"Let me get the cameras online. There. It's on your screen. Sun should set in about two hours. Winds gusting at up to forty-five miles an hour, and it's a balmy minus twenty Fahrenheit. Hope you brought a jacket."

"Where's that sandstorm Coop spotted?"

"On the other side of the planet. If it holds together, it won't be here for a couple of weeks. We'll be long gone."

"Planitia Base, this is General Carleton at Houston Control," erupted from the communication console. "Message received to general celebration." We could hear cheering in the background. "Congratulations, Lieutenant Colonel Gilmore, to you and your men. The entire planet is watching you with pride at this historic moment. I've just uploaded mission updates and personal messages from your families. We eagerly await your first Mars walk tomorrow. Contact us if you need anything. Houston over and out."

"Thanks, General. We got this covered. Planitia Base over and out." To us he said, "With the time to communicate with Earth, we are on our own. Everything by the book."

"I've got most of the cameras working, Cap," Toms said. "One aft is balky. I can take a look at it tomorrow. Exterior lights are on and I've got the link set on scroll. Everything being patched up to Coop."

Gilmore flipped his comm switch, "You reading, Coop?"

"Data coming in and recording. Great shots. We can make millions on postcards."

From my seat, I opened my computer screen, watching as the exterior view scrolled to a fresh scene every few seconds. The landscape, stark and barren, had a lonely beauty. Toms had found a level spot to land amid the rolling hills, rock formations and sand. Rusty sand everywhere, dotted with black rocks. The sky was a pale yellow, alien.

"I thought it would be redder," said Toms. "It's more yellowish than red out there."

"We're probably in a place where the silicate has a low iron content and didn't oxidize as completely. When we see the dunes in full sunlight tomorrow, they'll look red enough," I told him. *They told us all this in mission training, you ignoramus.*

"Okay, gentlemen. We have work to do. Burke, unpack the bins for tomorrow and make sure the collection packs are ready to go. Jeff, get down in the bay and make sure all launch systems are nominal. I'd hate to be ready to leave and no way to get back to the *Liberty*."

"Aye, aye, Cap." Toms got up and went to the hatch on the floor that I had just vacated. Our command module/return craft was in the 'golf ball.' An ungainly, faintly ovoid craft, just big enough for three large men, it sat atop the landing craft like a golf ball on a tee.

COOPER

I stretched my body and sank into the comfortable captain's chair, reveling in my solitude in the *Liberty*. Not only were Burke and the overgrown frat boys gone, but I had meaningful work after two months of tedium. All I had to show for the trip out was that it took the computer a few extra seconds to kick my butt at chess.

Gilmore, Toms and I had all been together for the experimental isolation work. Callahan was our fourth. We spent four months in Antarctica practicing the crowding and long days of minimal stimulation. It was as boring as Sunday afternoon at Grandma's house. At the two-month mark, the time it would take to get to Mars with our new quantum induction engines, the other three put on their suits and walked out on the glacier, just like a real Mars walk. We all survived relatively unscathed. But there was no way to compensate for one variable. We all knew that with the push of a button NASA could swarm in and rescue our asses if anything we couldn't handle came up. We had a net. Here, a hundred million miles from Earth, we were playing without that net. How do you train for that?

I had shaded my answers on my debrief. What else could I do? I had worked hard to join the Mars mission, harder than anyone knew. I had even used my expert electronic skills to hack into the NASA database and massage my test and interview scores. Not much. Just enough to give me a leg up on some others. This was my ticket. I didn't need to set foot on the planet to lay claim to having "been to Mars." Talk shows, a book, maybe even a movie. I was set to cash in. So I didn't say anything about Gilmore's power tripping and being a prima donna. I glossed over Toms' continuous feeding into it. I hoped Callahan would bring it up, but I couldn't queer my shot at Mars. Then Callahan was out, and Burke was in.

I pushed my hand through my sandy hair, checking my look on the computer screen. My hair had grown out in the two months since the NASA buzz cut. They gave us electric shavers and clippers and told us to maintain a clean-cut look for the media. Wanted us looking like all American boys. Gilmore had made us shave but did not enforce hair clipping. All of us were getting shaggy. Except old baldy Burke. *By the time we reach Earth in two months, my hair ought to be just right.* As the youngest member of the team at twenty-eight, I could play on my brashness. The media loved it, my publicist said. And when shaggy, I was the picture of youthful innocence. He said my easy good looks would make me a media darling.

BURKE

I hated Gilmore. Clear and simple. But I had to give him credit. He had such a presence that even without rank he would dominate any room. He was perfect for man's first step on another planet. His Nordic background came out in his blond hair and blue eyes, and his movie star good looks played well with the media back home.

Yeah, he's a perfect representative for the human race. The Aryan race. Can't let the first man on Mars be a colored boy like Toms or a Jew boy like me or a gay boy like Coop. No, NASA is still a racist good ol' boys' club.

I pulled out several implements we would need for Gilmore's walk tomorrow: hammers, picks, tongs, collection containers.

I'd been an outsider from the start. No, I wasn't in their isolation pod, but I did my own isolation with the alternate team. They should have scrubbed the entire alpha team when Callahan went down, but no, somebody had a hard-on for Gilmore, so I was just shoehorned in.

They'll be singing a different tune on the way back. I'll find evidence of the lost Martian civilization. Anyone who's looked at satellite pictures of Mars has seen the Face and the Pyramids. There must have been someone who built them. I'll be known forever as the discoverer of alien intelligent life in the universe.

COOPER

Stretched out in Gilmore's padded command chair, I had three computer screens angled to watch the spectacle. Best seat in the house. All that was missing was popcorn and a mint julep. I listened in on the comm unit.

"This is an historic moment, Lieutenant Colonel Gilmore. The world is watching. God be with you. Houston over and out." They had listened to the General's speech while donning the EVA suits; Gilmore taking his suit down from the wall rack first while Toms waited. Gilmore and Toms were going out.

"It's eight pm on the East Coast, bro. You know every TV in America, hell every TV on Earth is tuned in. All the networks," Toms said, a slight tremor in his voice showing his nerves. I knew he babbled when he was nervous.

"Yeah, we're stars. Think about that. And the women. No more getting shot down every night at the Pump House."

"Hey! I don't get shot down. Well, not much. But yeah. I'm a star now. Even being the second man on Mars ought to get me some action, talk shows, maybe a TV show. You got your pretty speech ready?"

Toms was shorter than Gilmore, but well-built from the workouts NASA required. His brown hair was hanging down his forehead and over his ears. It was a good look for him. His dark skin, straight hair and blue eyes took some getting used to, but he had been friendly with me. He blew hot and cold toward Burke, following Gilmore's lead.

"Yeah. The UN gave me some platitudes about world peace and claiming Mars for humanity. Sharing and shit. Yadda yadda."

"They ought to have you say what they really mean. 'We got here first. Fuck the rest of you'," Toms said.

"What about 'we come in peace'?" Burke interjected.

"Shit, when has that been true? We screw up every place we find," Toms replied.

"All right, turn your mic on now. Remember to keep it rated G. NASA rules," Gilmore instructed as he sealed his helmet.

Gilmore went through the airlock first. It was large enough to hold him, but nothing else. It wouldn't have fit the old-style EVA suits. The new suits were skintight, padded and unencumbered with outdated equipment. The breathing apparatus was no bigger than an ancient cell phone like my grandma once had. A chip in the suit interfaced with the ship's computer maintaining all systems.

Once the airlock had cycled, he opened the door and stepped out on the ledge and looked around. He was about three meters up. I was locked on the view from his helmet cam. Off to the right was an outcropping of rocks. They had identified that as the target of their second walk. To the left was sand. Rolling dunes, pink, rust, yellow led to a distant horizon. There was a thin atmosphere on Mars so there was sound, unlike on the Moon. His external microphone picked up the soft ticking of sand scraping across the landscape and around the landing module. The wind made a mournful whine as it passed through the nearby rock formation.

This is it. This is the money shot.

Gilmore turned and climbed down the steps of the ladder. The rocking of his head cam gave me a moment of vertigo. Then he set his right foot on the ground. He followed with the left. Once his feet were planted on the ground, he turned to survey the area.

The first man on fucking Mars!

Gilmore woodenly recited the speech they had given him. He waited while Toms exited the craft. Walking about was easy in the reduced gravity; the both of them walked as if there were springs on their feet. Gilmore pushed a flagpole deep into the ground. Toms helped him attach an American Union flag. The familiar red St Andrew's cross dividing a blue field spangled with sixty stars would flutter in the Martian wind. They had made it of metallic fibers that would withstand the constant scratching of the Martian sands in the ceaseless wind. At least for a while. They erected a second flagpole and attached the UN flag.

Gilmore walked about like my grandpa surveying his plantation. He stopped and examined each large rock he encountered. He turned and looked at the *Freedom*. It was squat like a giant four-legged spider wrapped in gold foil. With a golf ball on its back. It was the same type of craft they had used for the Moon shots a hundred years ago. His helmet view showed Toms inspecting the cameras and external sensing devices. Toms found the problematic camera and made repairs. A beep on my console alerted me it was time for our next act.

"Lieutenant Colonel, you have incoming on your left," I radioed into his helmet.

As he turned, I and about ten billion people back home saw a golf cart sized craft lumbering into view. It trundled up and stopped a few meters short of Gilmore.

"*Intrepid*! Nice to see you, old boy," Gilmore cried. The *Intrepid* was the latest Mars rover. It had caught the attention of the world last year as NASA milked a "will it or won't it survive a sandstorm" story. The little guy had Instagrammed his status every day. NASA had programmed it to rendezvous with us for maintenance and a photo op. After about forty-five minutes of what I considered dicking off, they returned to the landing craft.

BURKE

It's showtime! Today I make history. Or re-write it.

I felt an irrational fear of letting go of the bottom rung of the ladder after leaving the landing craft. Once standing on the ground, the fear abated, but the urge to barf only increased. Throwing up now in my helmet would be humiliating. *The entire world is watching.* Of course, that thought only increased the need to blow.

"You were right, Burke. It does look redder in the sunlight," Gilmore commented.

We worked our way to the black rock formation. I was giddy and wanted to test the gravity by seeing how far I could jump, but restrained myself. The outcropping was large, dozens of meters long, rising out of the sand like ruins I had seen in the Middle East. The irregular rocks towered over our heads, reaching ten meters or more.

Geology was my specialty, and I was excited to be given this opportunity. God knows I've earned it. I'm a damn good geologist and have kissed enough asses to get this. I've been passed over enough times by the brass. They almost passed me over for this trip because some fool bureaucrat thought forty-five was too old. *I'll show 'em all.*

I crouched to get a better look at the edge of the rock formation. It was sedimentary; could be an ancient seabed. There might be fossils embedded, so I took out my hammer and chipped off pieces into a specimen container.

"Burke, over here," Gilmore called.

When I joined him, he pointed out lichen growing on a rock surface. Probes had shown that lichen, mosses, and mold grew on Mars. Extreme biota for an extreme environment. But this was the first time we could get a sample to study. I scraped the lichen into a specimen container. This was a prize find. The guys back home could examine the DNA of the plant and compare it to Earth life.

"I'll take this back to the ship," Gilmore said. "You keep looking around."

"Sure, Cap."

COOPER

As required, I was streaming the Mars walk data back to NASA. I knew they'd be high as a Georgia pine that we collected a specimen of native life. The view from Gilmore's helmet bounced up and down as he loped back to the landing craft. With a faint "blip," I lost the video on Burke's helmet and an alarm began pinging that his blood pressure and breathing had spiked.

"Crap," I muttered as I tried to reboot his system. "Burke, what's going on? Can you talk to me?"

Nothing. I called Gilmore next.

"Cap. Cooper here. I've lost contact with Burke. His helmet cam went off. His vitals are elevated. He may be in trouble. Is he within visual?"

The panoramic sweep as Gilmore pivoted was dizzying. The helmet cam showed Burke running toward him. Again, with a "blip," Burke's mic popped back on. Still no visual.

"Lieutenant Colonel! You gotta come see. It's amazing. You gotta see."

"Calm down, Major. What is it?" Gilmore grasped Burke by his forearms to steady him when he arrived.

"A wall. I found a wall!"

"A wall? What do you mean?"

"It's ancient. Just a few mud bricks. But it is a structure. Or the remains of one. You gotta come see it. It's probably the most important find ever!"

Shit, Burke found a wall? I thought it was just a pipedream of his.

Gilmore followed Burke back to the rocks they had been examining.

"Over here," Burke said, leading him around several large rocks.

Through Gilmore's camera I saw small rocks strewn about as if someone had broken them up and scattered them.

"What?" Burke said, his voice going up two octaves, his hands up on his helmet. "It was right here. Something or someone must have destroyed it. It was right here."

"Okay, Burke. You got it on your helmet camera, right?"

"Helmet camera? Yeah, I got it there. Great. But I know what I saw. It was right here. Just a trace. Now it's gone. Something has destroyed it."

"Okay. I believe you. Gather as much as you can into a container. We can examine it later. I think we ought to get back to the ship."

I could pick up on Gilmore's unease as he waited for Burke to fill his container. On my private line, he asked if onboard infrared picked up any warm bodies other than he and Burke. I checked but knew at this distance it was useless. As they made their way back to the ship, I could hear over the comm channel Burke muttering "who would do such a thing" and "greatest find in history". I wasn't given to fancies, but what Burke said had triggered my military training. Down there, they were exposed.

BURKE

"Excursion over so soon?" Toms commented once Gilmore followed me through the airlock. "I was just chatting with Coop. He said y'all found something."

"Hey, Cap," Cooper called over the radio unit.

"Coop, keep the comm open. we need to talk. Burke says he found a formation that a few minutes later was altered by forces unknown. He thinks there may be something out there."

"I never said that, Cap. I'm not crazy. I saw the remains of a wall. And later it was destroyed. You can draw your own results. I'm not nuts enough to say it out loud." I wasn't about to let them throw me under the bus.

"The wind has pretty strong gusts. Maybe what you saw got blown over," Toms offered.

"It wasn't blown over. It was purposely destroyed." *Something doesn't want us to find evidence.*

"You seeing little green men, Burke?" Toms teased. "It's easy enough to prove. What does the helmet footage show?"

"Download his helmet data, Coop," Gilmore said. "Play it back on the screen here."

The scene was jerky as I was getting used to the gravity. As we approached the rock formation it smoothed out. Then the signal cut off.

"What happened?" Gilmore asked Coop.

We could hear Cooper clicking buttons for a moment.

"That's all there is, Cap. The video recording just shut off."

"Burke!" Gilmore said.

"I didn't do it, Lieutenant Colonel," I defended myself. "As far as I knew, my camera was working fine."

"Cameras don't just cut off," Toms said.

"Cap," Cooper interrupted them. "Re-upload the file to me. Make sure I get everything the helmet recorded. I'll be able to tease something out."

"From now on, helmet cameras are priority when on an EVA. Whoever we leave behind in the module will keep a constant eye on the units to make sure they are working at optimum. Understood? It'll be dark soon. Jeff, be sure all the floodlights are on and the cameras are working. Burke saw something and I don't like it."

•   •   •

In the hours just before dawn, I woke. On the other side of Gilmore, I saw Toms had his seat upright and was looking at his computer unit.

"What's up?" I whispered, not wanting to awaken Gilmore.

"Couldn't sleep. I guess you could say I'm keeping watch. In case any Martians attack."

"Not funny, Toms. I saw something." I didn't like being the butt of their sophomoric jokes.

"Sorry, guy. I don't mean nothing by it. Just razzing you. Man, it is desolate out there. A real desert. It would be a fucked-up place to live."

"I don't know," I said, tamping down my annoyance. "Throw up a little cantina and it would have a certain cachet."

"That it would, man. That it would."

I needed to stretch, so got out of my seat with minimal groaning. *He thinks I'm crazy. Seeing little green men. They're so macho but would piss their pants if they saw real evidence of a civilization. If they even recognized it, bonehead jocks.*

I groaned once more as I arched my back and stretched out my arms. I was turned to the wall, so my face was at a porthole. I watched the unending Martian wind blow sand across the landing site in the Martian dawn. It was beautiful and hypnotic.

That was when I saw it. The shadow.

"What was that?" I said louder than I meant. "I saw something. In the shadows out by the rocks."

"What? Ow, goddamn it!" Toms had banged his knee trying to scramble out of his seat. He limped over to the porthole. "What? What did you see?"

The commotion woke Gilmore.

"What's going on?"

"Burke says he saw something. Out there," Toms called over his shoulder.

"Burke. Talk to me," Gilmore ordered.

"Out by the rock formation, where I saw the wall. I looked that way and saw a shadow. It looked like someone was moving among the rocks. Furtive like."

"Are you telling me there are people out there?" Gilmore's voice was incredulous.

"No, Cap. I just know I saw some shadows."

"Jeff, pull up the surveillance cameras. What do they show?"

"The cameras aren't focused on the rocks. Just the landing site itself," Toms told him.

"Well, we've had two unexplained incidents in the rocks. Don't you think it's time we aimed a fucking camera at them?" Gilmore's usual calm voice was strained. His color was up, and I could see a vein pulsing at his temple. Gilmore was angry.

"Aye, Cap. I'll dedicate a camera to it," Toms replied.

COOPER

They briefed me on "the shadow" when I called for the morning check in. I told them I had parsed every byte of data from the headset to no avail. "It looks like someone just switched it off."

"I didn't fuck with my headset," Burke growled. I'm sure he thought we didn't believe him.

"No one's saying you did. Just simmer down," Gilmore said.

"I believe you, Burke," I said. "Those helmets get a load of sand and dust in them each time you go out. It's no wonder one of them went wonkers. It's my guess one of the fuses got fried. You were having trouble with it just before y'all went down. I can check it out when y'all get back up here."

"Well, we've got more footage from the night cameras," Gilmore said. "It should have uploaded automatically."

"Yeah, I saw it first thing. I'll analyze it. You guys are working hard and I'm sitting up here just jacking off. It'll give me something more productive to do with my hands," I said, laughing.

"You better not get any jism on my bunk," Toms yelled, also laughing.

"Naw, I'm hanging out in the luxury of the mission commander's quarters," I replied.

"I'll pretend I didn't hear that," Gilmore said.

I could see on my unit that Burke continued to brood, looking daggers at Toms and Gilmore. *I'm afraid there's a fire in Georgia on that horizon.*

Burke was still struggling to fit in with Gilmore and Toms. Those two were like an old married couple. They had been together so long they almost spoke their own secret language. I had tried to insert myself but couldn't break the barrier. Burke was also excluded, so he and I bonded. Burke enjoyed my wild tales of clubbing during my early twenties. I told him how I'd met my boyfriend, Tommy, and about our porn collection. I even offered to lend him a porno file. Burke related his staider upbringing. He was rigid, stayed within the lines, always conforming. He had decided that was the way to get ahead in the military.

I was all the more surprised when Burke later confided in me his belief that there had once been intelligent life on Mars. He cited the Great Face, the Pyramids and Temple ruins. I accepted the conventional wisdom that these were all conspiracy theory ideas, but Burke was a true believer. He hoped to uncover some archaeological evidence. I wished him well in his quixotic quest, but wondered how he'd slipped past the NASA personality tests. Maybe he knew a hacker, too.

•   •   •

I was still working on the data download a few hours later when I heard them talking down below. I synced one screen in case I needed to chime in.

"Cap, take a look at this," Toms said. I saw he had a still shot of the landing site on his screen. "The wind's a bitch out there and has a shitload of sand to play with.

It's like a mini sandstorm with the sand coming in sheets like rain in a downpour. Now look at this." He animated his screen in slow motion. "Here, several sheets of sand come off the desert and blast through our lights. See the shadows they cast? Looks like a man running across the site. The blowing sand is causing the shadows."

"I'll be damned. It does look that way. Burke, does this look like what you saw?"

Burke was quiet for a few moments, studying his screen. "Maybe. But it doesn't explain the wall or my unit failing."

"We've got an EVA this afternoon. I want to do some digging in the area you saw the wall. There should be more of it underground."

Burke offered Gilmore a small smile, looking grateful that he at least pretended to believe him. *Things are getting tense down there. They need to lighten up.*

BURKE

"Jeff, it's about time we got ready for the EVA. I'll suit up first," Gilmore said.

Once he was dressed, Gilmore moved to the airlock to give Toms room to change. I got up to give Toms an easier way out of the seats. As I was standing, I gazed out the porthole at the lonely planet. *There it is again!*

"There! I see it, a definite body," I shouted. Toms shoved his head up next to me.

"I see it, too. There is something out there," he confirmed.

Gilmore couldn't get to the port hole wearing his EVA suit. "Jeff. Suit up fast. I'm going out."

While he went into the airlock, I turned on a multiscreen display of their helmet cams and lander cams.

Gilmore waited at the bottom of the ladder until Toms joined him.

"I'll sweep the perimeter this way; you go the other way. Burke, keep this channel open, monitor both helmets and lock the hatch. I don't want anything getting in there but us."

"Me either, Cap," I responded, eyes wide.

Shit, maybe they're after us. What have we stumbled into? Maybe Toms and Gilmore will believe me now.

•   •   •

Gilmore rendezvoused with Toms at the ladder to the lander thirty minutes later. They had maintained near continuous verbal contact during their search. I heard little of it, sitting frozen in my seat, sweating bullets, desperately trying to cling to my sanity. *They are after us.*

"So, you didn't see anything?" Gilmore asked Toms.

"Nada. Just a whole lotta sand. You know, the more I think about it, the more I suspect maybe I was overexcited by Burke's yell, just saw a shadow of blowing sand," Toms said.

"All right, let's get inside. You go up. I'll bring up the rear." I could see through Gilmore's helmet cam as he watched Toms start up the ladder.

Toms was through the airlock first. The way he stared at me confirmed that I looked as bad as I felt. I was huddled in my seat, wishing I had room to put my head between my legs. The light in the cabin seemed preternaturally bright, and I was having trouble getting my breath. Toms didn't say anything; he just waited for Gilmore.

"I'm so glad you guys are back," I gasped. "Did you see the marks?"

"What marks?" asked Gilmore.

"Something was scratching at the door, like it was trying to get in."

"Why didn't you call us?" Gilmore asked, staring at me. I found it hard to meet his gaze.

"I don't know. It was like I couldn't." I lowered my head and stared at my lap.

"You mean you froze? Is that what you're telling me?"

"Yeah, I guess. It scared me. I was afraid it would scratch right through that door," I finished, knowing I'd failed again.

Gilmore grabbed my shoulders and shook me. "Get a grip, man. We got a situation here and I need all my officers working at top efficiency. If you want to piss your pants, do it on your own time. Right now, you're on my time, and when Jeff and I are outside, you're definitely on my time. We rely on you to have our backs. I expect you to sit up and remember you're an officer of Space Command. Do you understand?"

I nodded.

"I said, do you understand?" Gilmore reiterated.

"Yes, sir. I understand." I glared at Gilmore, thinking murderous thoughts, as I'm sure my face blazed red in embarrassment and anger.

"Coop," Gilmore called out.

"Yeah, Cap."

"Do exterior cameras show anything other than us approaching the vehicle door?"

"Nada, Cap," he answered after a pause.

"Review audio from interior. Any noises sounding like scratches on the door?"

Another pause.

"Shit! I mean affirmative. There is some noise in the background. It sounds like scratching."

"How about video?"

"Uh, the internal video surveillance isn't continuous. It wasn't recording at the time."

"Well, keep it the fuck turned on. Keep every fucking camera turned on every fucking minute. Goddamn it!" Gilmore roared.

I winced. *He's going to give himself a coronary at this rate. Good.*

"Aye, Cap," Cooper said.

"But, Jim," Toms interrupted. "There's two doors between here and the outside. The airlock is the only way in and both of them were closed during our EVA."

"Jeff, suit up. Go out and inspect both sides of both doors. I want to know if there are any marks. We're a hundred million miles from help, so we gotta take everything seriously. Coop, you monitor his cam."

COOPER

Gilmore opened our hastily convened meeting with a blunt, "I need to draft a message to Houston and get some guidance. We may be in danger sitting here like this."

"Come on, Jim. It's not like we've got any evidence. All we got is shadows. You call Houston, they're gonna think we're a bunch of old women having the vapors. Are y'all scared of a few shadows?" Toms was trying to be rational.

"Shadows don't scratch at doors," Burke said.

"Yeah, but neither door was marked," Toms said.

"Something made a noise and scared Burke," Gilmore said and looked over at Burke.

"Sorry, don't mean to talk about you like you aren't here."

"It's okay," Burke answered with no emotion in his voice.

"It's possible that something is out there. Until I know otherwise, we're operating as if we are at risk," Gilmore continued.

"Relay's open," I told him.

Gilmore sketched over what we had experienced so far. He ended by asking for guidance.

"General, I know there's a lot riding on this mission, but the safety of my men is my priority. We're up here with no weaponry, and something might be out there. Both my men have seen 'shadows' and I'm sending the imagery from the landing site for the NASA and I-MINT guys to analyze. Cooper can't find anything, but maybe your specialists can find something we're missing. I'm cautious about further EVAs until I know what we're facing, if anything."

Sixteen minutes later we received a terse transmission. "Twenty billion dollars riding on this. Proceed with caution."

"What the fuck is 'caution'?" Burke yelled. It seemed his patience was at an end. "Without weapons, we can't defend ourselves, and we don't know what's out there. But it wants in here. We need to get back up to *Liberty*." His color was up, he was breathing hard and sweat covered his face.

I worried that he was having a panic attack. It can happen when people are cooped up too long.

"Burke. Get ahold of yourself. You know our mission parameters. Houston wants us to stay. We'll collect our specimens, service *Intrepid*, and go. It's only three more days," Gilmore reminded him.

•　　•　　•

Since they were crammed in together, there was no way for private voice transmissions, but late that night my screen lit up with a typed query from Gilmore.

<Can lift off function of Freedom be controlled from Liberty? Jeff and I have an EVA tomorrow, and Burke might panic and lift off without us. I hope to get Burke on the EVA, but I doubt he'll leave the module. He's seriously on the verge of a breakdown. Can you override?>

I understood Cap's concern. The lander had enough fuel to land and return to orbit. It might be able to squeeze out another landing, but that would be a one-way trip.

<Sorry, Cap. They base all flight functions of the landing craft on your end. I just get to watch. I can initiate a launch like if y'all get incapacitated, but I can't retard one. But I can show you how to rig a false systems overload on the launch sequence. It won't launch during the overload but will reset itself in about an hour. Too bad about Burke.>

<He's been wound up tight the whole journey. I'm surprised NASA didn't pick up on it during personality testing. So how do I overload?>

BURKE

"Burke, I want you with me on the EVA today," Gilmore said.

"Why? What's wrong with Toms?" I couldn't help the panic I heard in my voice.

"I want you. I want to go do some digging where you saw that wall. I need your help."

"I don't want to go. Not out there. They're out there. They don't want us to find their wall. They're waiting for us." *Don't they get it? The EVA could be a trap.*

"Get a grip, Burke."

"No. I saw one again. Last night. I got a good look. They look like lizards, with greenish gray scaly skin." *I'll never forget that ugly face peering in the window as long as I live.*

"Did you get video?"

"No. They know where the cameras are and are avoiding them." *What's the use? I can tell from his tone he dismisses me. He dismisses everything I've said on this mission.*

"Then we need to get evidence of the wall to back up your story of the Martian civilization."

"No. I won't go." I began hyperventilating. My legs collapsed, and I fell back in my seat. I couldn't do it. I knew that if I left the lander, I might never come back.

"Cap," Toms broke in. "He's tired. I'll go with you." He put his hand on my shoulder. "You going to be okay when we get back, bud?"

I nodded, trying to get my breathing under control.

"Burke, I'm letting it go this time, but I need you to be a team member if we're going to get out of this. I'm cutting you no more slack. Have you assayed the mineral samples we collected yesterday?" Gilmore started pulling on his EVA suit.

When I told him I hadn't he suggested I occupy my time on the assays. *Instead of fretting like an old woman,* is what he meant.

"I'll wait outside," he told Toms and entered the airlock. "Cooper, monitor us."

Once Toms had exited the craft, they headed toward the rock formation. I was feeling on edge, off centered. Something was out there. I felt in my bones that something bad was about to happen. I saw no need to work on the mineral assays. Our time was limited.

COOPER

As I watched the EVA, Gilmore looked at Toms and held up two fingers low by his side, indicating channel 2, private communication on their headsets. I switched over to channel 2 to listen in.

"I'm worried about Burke," Gilmore said. "I don't need my crew having panic attacks. We're on our own out here. I even had Coop tell me how to override our engines so the ship can't take off for an hour. I'm afraid Burke could panic and maroon us."

"Cap. Jim, I feel it's partly my fault. I shouldn't have ridden him like I did. It didn't help matters. And my sighting yesterday. I'm not sure I saw anything. The more I think about it, it was just sand blowing in the wind. That's probably all Burke's seen. He's just so keen on finding a lost Martian civilization that he's conjured this all up."

"I think you may be right. All this excitement has just about pushed him into a psychotic break."

I beeped in, signaling Gilmore to switch over to channel 3, my private channel. He switched over. I locked it so no one but Gilmore and Toms could listen in.

"Coop. What's up?"

"Well, I hope you're satisfied. You probably just pushed Burke over the edge."

"Lieutenant! You're out of line."

"The hell with the line! I saw you signal channel 2 and if I saw it, that means Burke saw it. How much you wanna bet all four of us just listened in on that little chat?"

"Shit!"

"Shit is right. Both of you are to blame. Hell, probably all three of us. Y'all been treating Burke like a spotted coon dog since the mission began."

"That's enough, Lieutenant."

"Not nearly. Not even a beginning." I'd been watching this develop and felt guilty for never stepping in. I was sure there were times I could have eased the situation, but I just opted to go with the flow. *Go along to get along, isn't that what they say?*

"Cooper. Calm down. I'll deal with it," Gilmore assured me.

"Well, I was just chatting with our boy as you two were leaving and he sounded pretty jittery. Talking about little green men."

"He's at the breaking point. We all bear responsibility in this. He's conjured up his dream about Martians. It's all a figment of his imagination," Gilmore said.

"What about the door scratches? The audio?" I interjected.

"We had no video. Burke could have been making the scratching noise," Toms said.

"Well, I'd suggest y'all do whatever it is you do and get on back. He needs some serious hand holding."

"We're on it. Over and out."

•   •   •

I stretched, feeling my vertebrae crack and pop. *Ohhh that feels so good.* I had dozed off for a bit, brooding about Burke. I hated what we'd done to him.

My work screen readout showed I could play my 110th game of chess or watch "Leather Goddesses of Mars" again. *Since my buddies down below think they're seeing little green men, Martian dominatrix porn seems kind of apt.* Except these little green men came with big green dongs. This was courtesy of Tommy. He was a technician at Houston Control and had embedded it in a personal message that NASA allowed him to send. I missed Tommy so much and was looking forward to holding him when I get back home. I hit a key and brought up his picture in a corner of my screen. *Ah, Tommy. I miss you so much. You are home to me.*

Home. That word holds such meaning now. I miss it so. I miss the smell of a steak sizzling on the grill, the sound of Tommy's soft laugh tickling my ear, the way my stomach flips when he whispers the sexy things he's going to do to me, the taste of a margarita, the feel of sea spray on my body, or Tommy's gentle hand caressing my face; all the things that say home.

I enjoyed being with the others, but cooped up in this tin can with them for the journey out was a special kind of hell. And it would be just as bad going back. We each had a private closet, but other than that we were cheek by jowl with each other all the time. The last three days alone on the orbiter had been pure bliss. No desultory conversations. No BO but my own. *I might miss the guys by the end of the week, but for now I'm luxuriating in the pure perfection of quiet.*

A buzzer sounded, reminding me it was time to check in with the *Freedom*. I noted that the continuous feed had been interrupted. *That's not supposed to happen. Malfunction or did someone on the lander turn it off? Cap's gonna be furious.*

"How's it going down there, y'all?"

"Five by five, Lieutenant." Burke's voice was soft and measured, none of the jittery edge he'd displayed a few hours ago. The hairs at the base of my neck started prickling. Something wasn't right.

"Let me speak to the Cap."

"He's not here."

"Really? How about Toms?"

"He's not here, either. They're on EVA." Burke was quiet, calm. Almost serene. My heart rate spiked, but I told myself I was just tense from the earlier problems.

"But that should have been over hours ago."

"It was, but they went back out."

"Why wasn't I contacted? I'm supposed to be notified of all EVAs, especially unplanned ones. What are they looking for?"

"They didn't confide in me. They never do."

I was tiring of Burke's placid one liners. Then I saw something that made my blood run cold. I toggled my camera controller to focus on the wall behind Burke.

Three EVA suits hung on the wall behind him.

"Burke, where are they?"

"I told you they went out."

"Their EVA suits are on the wall behind you."

"Oh, I guess they forgot to put them on."

Trying not to panic, I engaged all the exterior cameras. On the view from the airlock toward the bottom of the ladder, Jim Gilmore lay in a heap in the rusty Martian dust. His mouth was open, and his eyes were bulging as if they might pop.

"What the fuck, Burke? Where's Toms?"

"Oh, he's down in the specimen hold." Burke giggled. "He's our newest specimen."

"But he's going to be all right, huh?" I asked, hoping Burke had some shred of sanity left.

"I'm afraid not. The green men are curious about our physiology. I opened up Toms so they could examine him."

"Christ Almighty, Burke! Are you nuts?"

"Don't call me that!" he shouted. "I'm not crazy. I had to get rid of them to make room in the *Freedom* return shuttle. The green men want to meet us all, including you. I have to come and get you and bring you down to see them. The lander only holds three, so I had to make room. They were conspiring against me and the green men, anyway. I was told to neutralize them."

I swiped at the sweat that had broken out on my face. My heart was racing so fast I feared it would burst.

"But Burke," I said, trying to sound rational. "If we go down in the *Freedom*, we won't have enough fuel to get back to the orbiter."

"That's okay. The green men want us to live with them. We should be in optimal position for me to blast off in about an hour. Then thirty minutes till I dock. See you then. Planitia Base over and out."

"Holy fuck," I cried to no one, grabbing my hair with both hands. "Oh fuck, oh fuck, oh fuck. He's coming for me? What am I gonna do?" I tried to remember our pre-flight trainings. We had multiple contingencies but not for one of us wigging out and killing half the crew. I needed to get this to Houston Control, pronto.

I opened a new channel on the communication device. I tried to still my voice but as soon as I started talking it cracked and wavered. *I'm a soldier. I'm not supposed to panic. But I'm not a grunt, I'm a scientist. This is just insane!*

"Houston Control. Mayday, mayday. This is Lieutenant Caleb Cooper on the Mars *Liberty* Orbiter. Mayday, mayday. Major Burke appears to have had a break with reality. He has killed Lieutenant Colonel Gilmore. I have visual confirmation. He reports that he has killed Major Toms and claims he is being influenced by Martians. In an hour he plans to lift off in the return vehicle to come for me. It will automatically dock. I can't keep him out. If he overpowers me, he wants to take me down to the surface. If I overpower him, what am I supposed to do with him? I have no way to contain him for two months. What the hell am I supposed to do? Kill him? Maroon him? I need some help here. *Liberty*, over and out."

I hit 'send'. Feeling small and isolated, I drew my knees up to my chin. I wrapped one arm around my legs and gnawed on my thumb, shudders intermittently running through my body. A lone tear streaked down my cheek. The same thoughts ran over and over in my head. *Oh shit, he's coming for me. I gotta kill him. But I got no weapons. And he's Burke, my Burke. I can't just kill him. Can I? For a hundred million miles in all directions, there's only me and a madman. I'm so frigging scared.*

I watched the chronometer. At eight minutes, I knew Houston would have my message. It seemed like the longest eight minutes of my life. How long would they take to relay a plan? The waiting was killing me. The suspense might take me out before Burke could. As the chronometer hit sixteen minutes, my eyes focused on the comm device, never wavering. The hair on the back of my neck stood on end. My body was drawn tight as a bow. At sixteen minutes twenty-five seconds, the comm device beeped.

"Gaa!" I shouted at the startled release of the pent-up energy.

"Stand by," came the General's voice. *Yes!* They were working on a plan to save me. Ten interminable minutes later, the comm device beeped again.

"Lieutenant Cooper, we regret that you find yourself in such a grave situation. Off the record, son, you are in a helluva mess. I cannot authorize officers to kill other officers. That's not how things are done. And we do not maroon our astronauts. The public wouldn't stand for it, and it's immoral. Here is our press release: 'At 14:28 GMT, the *Liberty* Orbiter craft detected an explosion on the surface of Mars. Telescopic images from a low altitude flyover revealed a large debris field and nothing but the wreckage of the *Freedom* lander. All personnel, Lieutenant Colonel Jim Gilmore, Major Jeffrey Toms and Major David Burke are presumed to have died in the line of duty. Surviving crewmember Lieutenant Caleb Cooper was ordered to abort the mission and return to Earth. NASA is investigating the cause of the explosion.'

"That's the official report. By the time this reaches you, we will have initiated the self-destruct of the *Freedom* base. We program that in all NASA craft to prevent our tech falling into the wrong hands."

What the fuck? I've been sitting on a case of dynamite? What the hell?

The General continued, "We have programmed your ship to do a flyover to gather the photos I referenced. Now someone wants to say a few words."

"Caleb. It's me, Tommy."

"Tommy?" I leapt toward the comm unit, seeking something to hold on to. "Tommy, is it really you? Oh, Christ, I need to hear your voice right now." When Tommy continued as if I hadn't spoken, I reminded myself that Tommy wouldn't hear my words for another eight minutes.

"We're bringing you home, baby. Don't worry about a thing. We've got you covered. We can control the *Liberty* from here. All you need to do is relax and dream about home. The General has authorized unlimited face time with me for the duration. We'll get you back safe and sound. You know I wouldn't let you get away that easily."

"Lieutenant, this is General Carleton again. Officially, a grieving planet thanks you for your heroic service to your fellow officers and to all humanity. I think a field promotion is in order, so Captain Caleb Cooper, let's get you the hell out of there. Come on home, son. Houston over and out."

"Yes, sir!" I gasped and hit 'send.' Relief flooded my body. And then remorse at feeling anything but grief over the murders of Gilmore and Toms. And Burke. *We murdered Burke just as surely as he murdered the others.*

Even though I didn't push the destruct button, I knew I'd long carry a weight of guilt in the death of a man who I'd once considered a friend. And the field promotion was just a sop to remind me I was never to speak a word of this to anyone.

Just as the ship veered from its course and dove lower into the Martian atmosphere, I opened a channel to the *Freedom* lander.

"Burke. You still there?"

"I'm here, Cooper. Coming up on time for our rendezvous. I got anxious and launched a bit early. Good thing, too. Looks like something happened to the landing unit. That's okay. The green men will give us a place to land. I should be there in under twenty minutes."

"I've got orders to leave, Burke. Don't try to come up to the *Liberty*. It won't be here, and you won't have enough fuel to get back. You'll crash."

"You'll wait for me, Cooper. I know you will. You're my buddy. The green men told me you would wait. See you soon."

"Goodbye, Burke. I'm leaving now. Over and out."

I hit 'close' on the comm unit. Other than profound sadness, I felt little else, except a gentle thrumming in my padded seat. The ship flew over the landing site collecting pictures. Then it began its ponderous turnabout for the long, lonely journey home. Looking out the port I thought I saw in the distance the sun glint off the rising *Freedom* lander. It faded as I sailed on.

"God rest ye, old buddy."

ABOUT THE AUTHOR

Curtis Bass has more than twenty-five stories appear in online and print venues including *Youth Imagination*, *Page & Spine*, *Fabula Argentea*, a best of 2020 short story anthology, two horror anthologies, and two upcoming young adult anthologies. Curtis enjoys writing because he can let his mind wander free and never knows where it might end up.

YOU MIGHT ALSO ENJOY

HOT DROP
by J Dark

What starts as a rescue mission in a combat zone on a hostile planet becomes something more.

ONCE UPON A NIGHTWALKER
by Ryan Southwick

Ellen Bloom just wants a normal working relationship with her colleagues at her old job. But, at this point, she'd be happy with a pulse.

REDUCTION IN FORCE
by Steve Soult

A heartless corporate layoff leaves Gil Schaffer emotionally shattered. A revolutionary procedure may be his only hope for salvation, but the price could be greater than he bargained for.

Available in digital and trade paperback editions from
Water Dragon Publishing
waterdragonpublishing.com

www.ingramcontent.com/pod-product-compliance
Lightning Source LLC
Chambersburg PA
CBHW030826200726
48288CB00004B/1420